SALLY CINDERELLA

Other Clipper Street stories are:

CALLING FOR SAM

TALLER THAN BEFORE

ALL I EVER ASK...

A CLIPPER STREET STORY

SALLY CINDERELLA

Bernard Ashley

Illustrated by Judith Lawton

ORCHARD BOOKS

ORCHARD BOOKS
96 Leonard Street, London EC2A 4RH
Orchard Books Australia
14 Mars Road, Lane Cove, NSW 2066
ISBN 1 85213 873 4
First published in Great Britain 1989
First paperback publication 1996

A CIP catalogue record for this book is available from the British Library.
Printed in Great Britain

Contents

Sally never seemed right, never looked up to very much. Some people have the knack of looking good all the time—every day Queen of the May. They might be dressed in old clothes and climbing out of a pig sty but they somehow sparkle and smile, their eyes come through, and you can always take a photo you'd like to keep. Handsome. Pretty. Really up to the mark.

But others could spend a year in front of a mirror and they still wouldn't get a stare from a cat. Perhaps it all comes from inside: and there are some people who feel so miserable most of the time they don't care whether they're walking to a party—or off the nearest bridge. And Sally Lane knew more about pavements than she did about the sky, knew tree roots better than the leaves. A smile for her would have worked muscles that hurt. It wasn't the same for her sisters—it wasn't the same for the dog—but that's how it was for Sally.

She was up and dressed and down at the shop before most of the others had opened their eyes.

"Fags," her mother said one morning, "an' sugar." She gave her no money, just pressed her pencil message into a soft piece of card-board: soft looking words, hard heart, because her mother knew that certain stupid people felt sorry for Sally Lane. She was always the one to send when she wasn't going to pay.

Mrs Vasisht was one of them: and so was Kompel, who helped in the shop when she wasn't at school. Sally was only six but everyone seemed to know her.

"Yeah?" Kompel asked as the thin little girl slid in round the door.

Sally gave up the note, her eyes as usual on the floor. Kompel took it gently—because a quick moving arm would make her flinch, she knew.

"Hang on. I'll have to ask."

Sally waited. She was used to this. Not paying usually meant a bit of fuss. She yawned, eyed the fresh bread, smelt its heat.

"Sorry, tell your mother no cigarettes." Mrs Vasisht had come out. "Sugar O.K., but no cigarettes." She waved her fingers in a

"no" sign. "Cigarettes only for grown-ups. Little children not allowed." The shopkeeper's face was unsmiling, but then she was unsmiling with everyone, she wasn't picking on Sally.

Kompel gave Sally the smallest packet of sugar on the shelf. "It's the law, Sal," she explained. "See? My mum and dad gets into trouble if they sell cigarettes to kids…"

Sally stared at her, took back the cardboard note with *cigarettes* crossed through, walked out of the shop. She sighed as she went and her steps were slower than they had been coming. Slower steps, faster heart—because going home without the full message meant she'd done wrong. And doing wrong always got her a good hiding…

Kompel may have been hard worked, but she had never been hard hit. Working hard in the shop was natural, was expected. You didn't sit and watch much telly when your dad was stuck behind a Post Office grille all day and only came out on short visits: when your mum kept the shop doors open all the time there was light in the sky. Everyone in the family worked. Even little Sunil had to carry cola bottles and jump his frail weight on cardboard boxes.

But no one ever got hit. Dad might hold your hand hard, or look at you that sad way.

But hard hitting was for ants, and beetles, and mice. And the only other sort was for backs, soft pats, when people were pleased with you.

Kompel worked hard in school, too. She was good at maths because maths was what she *had* to know. Weights and litres and money—checking the red numbers on the till with her brain for homework, getting the change correct. And that helped to make school a good place to go. To get things right, to draw and dance and write poetry: all of which came from inside, from the energy of the sun that seemed to shine within her.

On the morning of the cigarettes Kompel got to the playground just before the bell, didn't have time for a game with anyone. But she did see Sally Lane, standing on her own over by the kitchen—watching her sisters playing chase.

Kompel shrugged. *No cigarettes* wasn't

down to her, was it? She couldn't make everything right for Sally. And she definitely couldn't make Sally's sisters play with her.

The bell was just about to go—and so was Kompel when Sally stared over at her and suddenly twisted herself away again. A sort of, "*You!*" look. "*You!*"

Well, it wasn't my fault! Kompel told herself. I'm sorry—but I didn't make the law about selling cigarettes. All the same, it had annoyed her, little Sally's huff. She felt *sorry* for her, she didn't deserve that sort of a look.

The first bell went, and most people stopped. Then the second, and they started going in. The runners who thought they couldn't be

seen, the walkers who hoped they could, and the have-another-kick boys who didn't care one way or the other.

Sally, being good, pulled herself off her wall and came towards Kompel. And Kompel, a monitor and expected in last, stood there and stared at her.

What was that? Sally looked different somehow, even to this morning. She wasn't

the same as when she'd come into the shop before school. Not quite. Something was different about her. Around the face.

Her cheek was swollen. She'd got a red, fiery mark under her eye, and she'd been crying.

"Wassup, Sal? What you done?"

But Sally barely gave Kompel the time for an answer. She hurried on past, her eyes on the grey of the ground. "Door swang back," she said.

And that was all. No being cross with it, the way people are.

And definitely no details.

Kompel had another good day. She was in on a few laughs, wrote a long piece about the month of May, won at volley-ball. She should have gone home happy. But somehow she didn't, couldn't—and Sally Lane was the cause of that. Her bad face had stayed with Kompel all day.

Poor little kid, she thought, being sent to school with a hurting face. No ointment on it. No plaster. Not seen to, probably, because they were cross with her over going home without the fags. By playtime one of the Helpers had put cream on it, but that wasn't

the same as having her mum or her dad look after her, was it?

Kompel got home and turned-to in the shop. They were always busy with kids after school, tons of them, buying penny chews and picture cards. You needed eyes everywhere: more like being a teacher than a shop keeper. But, as her mum said, don't look down your nose at it. It was all the cheap bits, the small packets which kept the corner shop going.

They all went to *Asda* for their big stuff; and came here for what was handy. And for the "slate", when they weren't going to pay.

The slate was the book where Kompel's mother wrote what people owed. People with regular business at the Post Office counter could run up little bills—then on paying-out day they had to settle.

And being Thursday, Mrs Lane came in for the Post Office, after the main rush.

No one could tell how hard she was on Sally, not by looking at her. She seemed an ordinary sort of person, not some cruel witch. She'd got little Lindy with her, and she bought her a Twix, stroking the kid's white blonde hair, settling up her bill like Lady Muck.

"Sorry about cigarettes," Kompel's mother said to her. "We're having to be very careful right now."

"Oh, that's all right, love. Just can't start a day without a fag, can I, Lind?"

Lindy shook her head as if it were a known fact, like those you learned in school. Important.

"Fag an' a cough get me going."

If you asked her, Kompel couldn't tell what made her say what she did. All she knew was that she suddenly heard herself saying it—with a somersault in her stomach to tell her she was really taking a chance.

"Shame about Sally's face," she said.

Mrs Lane turned and stared at her, cold. It was like looking into the face of some dangerous animal which might suddenly spring, and bite you.

"Yeah!" she said. "Clumsy little cat,

weren't she, Lind? Fell down the steps."

Lindy nodded: didn't bat an eye.

Mrs Lane's voice was flat and freezing. Lindy's eyes were like ice. But the real chill was in Kompel's stomach.

Falling down the steps wasn't what Sally had said. "*Door swang back*," had been her words. Different stories. And neither of them was the truth, Kompel guessed. Because to be honest with herself, she'd known all day, hadn't she? Little Sally Lane hadn't had an accident. She'd been punched, like an enemy.

"You don't get involved in all that," Kompel's mother told her late that night. And her father made that clicking noise in his throat which said he agreed with her. "It's bad business to tell tales on customers. People soon stop coming in if they think we're secret police."

Three sentences, quickly spoken: but adding up to a terrible moment for Kompel. One she'd probably remember all her life. She'd remember the meal they'd just had and where all the things were on the table. Because it was the first time that she knew her parents were in the wrong, putting the family in front of what was right.

"How do you think it looks, eh, if an Indian family reports on them for cruelty, for this child abuse? How long before a brick comes through that window?" Her father's eyes seemed bigger than ever, his own skin more pale from the long days in his Post Office cell.

"An' how do you think it feels to have a punch in the face—and no one cares?" Kompel had never answered him back before. "She's a little kid—she's six!"

"The school will know. They don't shut their eyes to things like that."

"Not like you do, you mean!" Kompel got up and ran to her room. Angry. Crying. But leaving a long silence behind her which said they knew she was right.

The bruise on Sally's face got better, and quite quickly—almost as if the stares which Kompel gave her were some sort of ointment. And looking, smiling, saying something nice was all Kompel could do not to feel helpless.

She would have liked to do more, but there wasn't really the chance. She would have liked to make sure Sally never went home without her full message, for a start. She would have liked to talk to Sally about that bruise, if ever she could find a way: just to let her know that someone cared. And about the rest of it all. Kompel had never seen anyone who looked so unhappy all the time, in among a family of kids who laughed and played and looked all right. Out at play in Clipper Street, up at the top end where the cars couldn't go, they'd all be there with the others. But Sally would be talking to a wall or crouching to an ant, out of it, silent, while the rest made more noise than a treeful of starlings.

“Here, what’s up with Sally?” Kompel asked her little brother Bobby, who was still fat with paddi-pants and too young not to talk. “She a naughty girl indoors?”

“Naughty!” he nodded his head fiercely. “Won’t go a-sleep. Nick the biscuits.” His little face was overtaken with the horror of it, and the hatred.

“Oh.” Kompel pretended to understand. Then, in a low voice so that his sisters wouldn’t hear, “Gets smacks, does she?”

Little Bobby looked at her: his lips went all stiff with the seriousness of Sally having to be smacked all the time for being so naughty. And he suddenly turned and toddled away—as if the family silence about smacks was something he'd just that second understood.

From now on Kompel had an aim in life. To make Sally Lane smile. It wasn't a great aim, not a changing-the-world sort of thing, not even a medium aim like changing Sally's family for a nicer one. But just this small aim of changing the look on Sally's face for a second or two.

She gave the girl sweets. She found a packet of picture cards with the wrapper torn and took them to school for her. She tried to get her into a game. But it was somehow as if Sally suspected that Kompel was trying to unlock her secret—as if she was scared of something worse which might happen if she did. And she wouldn't give an inch: not a millimetre of a smile. She took what was given to her and went back inside herself, staring at the lower half of the world with eyes which never shone.

In the classroom, though, where Kompel didn't see her, Sally played a clever game. She behaved more like the rest: she answered a few questions, read her reading book, played with the dolls when she got the chance. (And smacked them a lot for being naughty.) She was like someone who didn't want to stand out—except still she never smiled.

Kompel got nowhere near her aim. And, what was worse, one morning she really let Sally down. Right in the middle of her get-a-smile campaign, Kompel did the unforgivable. She switched off her alarm and turned over in

bed. And was cross with herself when she found out from her mother that Sally had been into the shop.

"Mrs Lane, she skipped out pretty quick yesterday. Didn't settle up. And this morning she sends for a list as long as you like. No money again! All on the slate!"

"Who came?"

"That one. Little Sally."

“What did you do?” If ever Kompel had needed to be there to make it all right!

“I gave her cornflakes and milk for the breakfast. For the children. But I told her, send her mother in to see me for the rest.”

Kompel kept her mouth shut tight, didn’t make a row again. After all, what else would she have been able to do that was better? Just made sure the cigarettes were in, for Mrs Lane’s morning cough? Yes! She’d definitely have done that, if she’d been about. That would have helped. And it was a warm summer morning, no need to have turned over in bed...

It went on to be a very hot day: like being on the equator. The first really hot day of the year in school and it was cotton dresses on for the girls, tee-shirts off for the boys, and pushing for drinks at the water taps. The cooks came in moaning about the heat as if they'd been putting up with it for weeks. And Mr Ransom drove his car in slowly with the top down...

In all of which Sally Lane wore a long-sleeved woolly cardigan. The rest of London was fanning itself in the hot still air and Sally Lane was dressed for the cold.

"You all right, Sal?" Kompel looked hard at the girl's face. But Sally's eyes said she couldn't trust her kindness: she couldn't afford to let anyone feel sorry for her. She stared back at Kompel, and walked on away.

"I only asked!" Kompel exploded. And then felt sorry. Didn't Sally get enough of the rough end of tongues?

It was one of those days that could have been bad tempered all round. In Assembly all the windows had to be open and London came roaring in. The push, push, push of the traffic, the throaty drone of the low level aircraft coming in to land at Heathrow. It was too hot to sing very well, and the announcements were given in the gaps between the heavy lorries. It would have been in and straight out except for one thing. Infants' May Day, coming up the week before half term: dancing round the May Pole and crown-

ing the Queen of the May. And today the names came out of the hat. The May Queen and the May Prince, chosen by chance from the Infants' top class.

Mrs Peters was there with the two cardboard boxes (no one had a hat). A big "Q" marked the Queen box, a big "P" the Prince.

The Juniors were hot and bored, but this was a big moment for the thirty top Infants, and everyone was shushed to sit ready to clap the lucky two. Kompel remembered. It would be a big day for them when it came. The procession, the crowning, the local paper with the big camera and all the parents with theirs. A day of being special, of fame. She hadn't had it herself, but she could remember

the thrill of it for Wendy Dorsett, whose smile hadn't faded for a week.

"So who are the two going to be?" Mrs Peters was asking. "Well, today we're going to find out!"

Twenty-nine straight backs, twenty-nine bright faces with tight smiles. And Sally Lane, hunched in her cardigan, sucking her thumb.

Everyone waited.

"And in Clipper Primary School tradition we'll ask two Year Six leavers to pull out the names. A big boy and a big girl," she explained for the Infants. "Let's see now..." Mrs Peters squinted to the back of the hall for a couple of good faces. "John Lunn...and... Kompel Vasisht."

With heavy sighs of responsibility John and Kompel pulled themselves up and stepped over to the front. And even something like that got your heart beating, Kompel found, even in your own school. All the eyes! But in a couple of minutes she was going to find her heart beating a lot harder still...

John Lunn was efficiency itself. When your father was a river pilot and your mother was a teacher you didn't need too much telling how to do such things. In went his hand and out came, "Sullaiman Shamime"—said very confidently.

"Thank you, John."

Two hundred heads craned and twisted to find Sullaiman—who was the one Infant suddenly interested in the velcro on his trainers.

"So Sullaiman's our May Prince this year. And..." Mrs Peters smiled all round, and she nodded at Kompel. The hall was very hot now. *Let's get this over and get out*, she seemed to be saying, one old hand to another.

Kompel's fingers dipped into the box Mrs Peters was holding above her. And it was then, in a sudden pound, that her heart knew what her head was going to do. And her head went all swimmy as she did it: as she tried to make everything up to Sally Lane: to bring the ghost of a smile to her sad face, just for a second. As Kompel's hand came out of the box she saw her, the hunched-over kid who thought she was no part of anything like this.

Marcia Knowles was the name written on the paper in beautiful italic. And *Sally Lane* was the name Kompel read out—with hardly a falter, nearly as well as John Lunn had done.

It was as if she'd pressed a small button: a faint-sounding buzzer going there in the hall. Teachers looked at one another and said things with their eyes. The other Lane children looked as if they'd drunk medicine. Someone coughed.

And Mrs Peters, in that electric moment, asked to see the piece of paper. "May I?" she said, in the voice she used when she was checking work you'd marked yourself.

Looking away, Kompel gave the paper to her. She had to give it, there was no alternative—she was like a prisoner who had to stand up straight in court while the damning evidence was read. She'd been so stupid! Why had she let herself get carried away?

She had always been trusted, the teachers liked her, and the little kids thought she was grown up, what with the shop and everything. And now she was going to look like the biggest cheat going.

Mrs Peters read the name on the paper to herself. She stared at Kompel. And she straight away said, "Thank you, Kompel. And well done, Sally, you'll make a good May Queen." She screwed the paper into her pocket and started the clapping—a movement of the air in the hall coming just soon enough to stop Kompel from fainting.

And still Sally didn't smile. She just stared up at Kompel and sucked harder on her thumb.

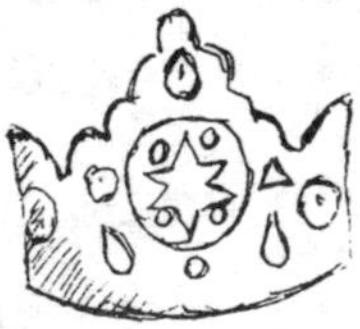

There was no inquest over it. No more was said. Perhaps Mrs Peters didn't know how to deal with such a thing—Kompel showing everyone how she felt about little Sally. One thing was certain: Kompel was sure the other teachers never knew. No one ever looked at her any differently for pulling that name from the hat. But whatever Mrs Peters did or didn't do, Kompel wouldn't have known anyway, because that went on in the private way things do in the staff room.

Each class teacher was organising their own different dance for the day. Mrs Gullivar was seeing to the Prince and his crown and robes. And Mrs MacKay, the deputy head, was in charge of the costume for the Queen—the dress for Sally to wear.

"I'll see how it fits," she said. Every year there were alterations to be made. The crown never needed to fit any better than the real Queen's, crowns just need careful balancing, but the dress had to be up to the mark.

Mrs Walker pulled a snobby face. "Uggh! I don't know how you can bear to touch that child!" She drove in from Kent each day to teach at Clipper Primary. "I'd be washing my hands for a week!"

Mrs MacKay half ignored her. "Oh, she's not so bad, poor little devil," she said, whisking the dress out of the staff room smoke; only her blotchy neck showing her anger.

Sally Lane had been kept behind in her classroom. Sullaiman Shamime was finished and gone, his Prince's robes hanging up like a giant puppet.

"Now then, let's see..." Mrs MacKay said. She held the shiny pink dress up to Sally. "Stand up straight, love."

Sally looked at her warily, some great fear behind her eyes.

"Looks all right for length. Perhaps we'll turn the hem just half an inch." The hem went up and down regularly, had as many needle holes as it had material. "Now, do we need a tuck in the back?" Mrs MacKay could have been talking to some forlorn little statue. "I hope you'll give us a May Queen's smile on the day, eh? Mummy *will* be pleased." But it was just words. They both knew the game that was being played—pretend, pretend, pretend. "Now, cardy off—we shan't have that on, on the day..."

But now the statue moved. Sally drew back, resisted, and spoke. "Mustn't," she said. "My mum told me." She was gripping the bottoms of the cardigan arms with her small, chewed fingers. "I got a cold."

"Oh, come on. It's a lovely hot day. I'll

take the blame!" And like the firm mother she was herself, Mrs MacKay had the cardigan off. "One, two, three!"

While *four* and all the way to twenty was silent at the sight of Sally's arm. Where a bite, a red and white human bite, told its own terrible story.

"How did this happen?" Mrs Peters asked her kindly, in her room. "Who did this to you?"

Sally Lane stared sullenly at the floor.

"Eh?" the headteacher asked, as if Sally had answered and she just hadn't heard. "Sally—how did this happen?" She waited, patiently, with just the raising of her eyebrows.

There was a long, long wait.

"Come on!" she said, just a bit more sharply.

"King," Sally murmured. "Our dog."

"Oh, King! But his mouth's not this shape, is it? A dog's mouth is different altogether. Lovie, I can see the tooth marks..."

"Didn't anyone treat it?" Mrs MacKay asked. "No *Savlon*?" She dropped her voice. "And what about your bad face the other day?"

But Sally was back to staring. They knew. Her eyes, suddenly sharp, said it all. The game was up—her mum's and dad's game—but she didn't want to get worse done to her for saying...

"This is a...person's...bite, Sally. And a big person's. Now, who was it? We've got to know, you'll have to tell someone..."

No amount of cajoling or explaining got another word out of her, though. No amount of being made to feel safe. No amount of telling how the school *had* to ring Social Services, and how Social Services *had* to look into it. Sally clammed right up, as if being forgiven for not telling was the last little thread of hope she had to hold on to.

The woman from Social Services was very kind—Ms Partridge, to be called Penny. She came quickly and she took Sally home to her parents. She showed them Sally's bad arm; and, very quietly, she wanted to know how it had happened.

The children were sent to play out at the back, and in a calm, friendly, firm way she let them know what the score was. What her powers were. How her office knew where she was and how they needn't bother shouting or abusing or threatening. All they had to do was tell her.

She made it clear that Sally herself had said nothing, except to blame the dog: but that no one had believed that, and they certainly wouldn't when a doctor took a look at that arm. She also set the school's part of it straight: they hadn't poked or pried, it was all over the May Queen, as simple as that.

"May Queen!" Brian Lane suddenly broke his fierce silence. "Ain't they s'posed to *teach* 'em? May Queen!" He looked as if he had a lot more shout in him, too, but his wife gave him a look and he shut up. Left his leg dangling over the arm chair to show whose house it was.

Very matter of fact, puffing smoke, Sally's mother went through different stories of the bite. The dog, it *must* have been: Sally often annoyed him, which is why she hadn't shown them her bad arm. Or if it was human it had to be a big kid at school: there was a lot had it in for Sally. And how did they know it wasn't a teacher? God, some of the teachers *she'd* had as a kid! Half killed you and nothing got said.

But Ms Partridge had an answer to everything. The shape of the bite. The size of the different tooth marks. How a doctor and a dentist could match it with the mouth that did it—and would, if need be. She ran the Lanes into dead ends, to places their stories couldn't go—till anger and frustration suddenly had Brian Lane bursting out with the truth.

"All right! I done it!" he shouted. "Cleverpuss, ain't you? You don't know her, the little madam! She's trouble from the minute she wakes up to the minute she goes to bed!"

"Gave me a bad time from the off," his wife said, patting her stomach as if Sally had committed some crime in the womb. "Could be her middle name, Trouble. Never stopped crying, gave us a hell of a time, broken nights..."

"She gets fed proper, gets dressed nice. Then it's always after more—want, want, want. Lies. Steals. You need a lock on that fridge. Took the dog's dinner once..."

"A right little cat. There's no pleasing her..."

Ms Partridge kept her eyes down and took some notes, matter of fact.

But she wasn't the only one listening. Sally was outside the door, listening to her parents listing their love for her. And her eyes glazed over, as if even the painful bite couldn't hurt hard enough to keep her sharp. As if nothing could hurt very much against the Council being told all this...

Kompel never knew quite what happened. Some true stories aren't wrapped up in endings for everyone taking part in them to read. She'd never actually known about the arm: not even all the teachers had known about that. And she didn't know about Social Services, nor how the school had only been waiting to jump onto something certain before calling them in.

But she did see something of the change she'd made by reading that false name from the hat, although she never knew it had anything to do with her.

All at once there were new dresses for everyone to see. And Sally walking with her sisters—and not being the one who did all the messages while the rest of them laid in bed.

And she was the May Queen, with her

mother coming to clap her, all on her best behaviour. Sally Lane did that ever so well, Kompel thought—went through all the right moves and remembered where to stand. Almost smiled when a footballer put the crown on her head; was very special for a day.

But Kompel never knew who helped to make sure it happened. Further up Clipper Street, though, some of the neighbours knew Ms Partridge and what she did. They saw the regular car outside, noticed how the shouting from the Lanes' house got quieter, except when it was, "Sally, *love*," all very loud and clear.

And from behind their net curtains some of them knew about the deals Social Services did with people like the Lanes. *We'll help out, but only if you try.* We're keeping a good eye on you, and one step out of line, one more bruise or burn or bite or stripe and we'll throw the book at you—and see the mark *that* makes!

They knew Sally understood. How she was on a deal, too. A deal to tell. There were to be no more dark secrets, not any more. She even had a number to ring.

And all at once, she had the power. She could get what she wanted some days with no more than a hard stare at the others. Things like biscuits, and sweets, and she even got to see what she wanted on the television. Well, the neighbours said, after what she'd been through, didn't she deserve it?

But there wasn't any deal on love. Social Services couldn't quite make that happen.

Kompel worked on in the shop and she saw Sally Lane come in and go out, growing up, looking more and more people in the eye every day: even got given a hard look herself when she didn't get round to serving the girl fast enough. And once she heard Sally swearing at her father behind his Post Office grille. But she pretended not to see, not to hear. How could the girl know what was normal?

Kompel never regretted what she'd done that day in Assembly. And she would always be grateful to Mrs Peters for making it her secret, too. Because didn't you have to help

Cinderellas like Sally? Make allowances for them?

And just hope that one day they might get the chance to start living happily ever after...